P9-ARR-805

NYACK LIBRARY
59 South Broadway
Nyack, NY 10960

Everyone Wins at
TEE BALL

Henry and Janet Grosshandler

900914

COBBLEHILL BOOKS
Dutton • New York

NYACK LIBRARY
59 South Broadway
Nyack, NY 10960

Copyright © 1990 by Henry and Janet Grosshandler
All rights reserved
No part of this boook may be reproduced in any form without permission in writing from the
publisher

Library of Congress Cataloging-in-Publication Data
Grosshandler, Henry.
    Everyone wins at tee ball / Henry and Janet Grosshandler ; photographs by the
authors.
        p.   cm.
    Summary: A simple introduction to the rules and techniques of T-ball.
    ISBN 0-525-65016-4
    1. T-ball—Juvenile literature.   [1. T-ball.]   I. Grosshandler, Janet, ill.   II. Title.
    GV881.5.G76   1990
    796.357'62—dc20   89-7875
                                                                                          CIP
                                                                                          AC

Published in the United States by E.P. Dutton,
a division of Penguin Books USA Inc.
Published simultaneously in Canada by
Fitzhenry & Whiteside Limited, Toronto
Designed by Jean Krulis
Printed in Hong Kong
First Edition   10   9   8   7   6   5   4   3   2   1

For Nate, Jeff, and Mike,
who have shown us how to be
good sports

NYACK LIBRARY
59 South Broadway
Nyack, NY 10960

Boys and girls who are six, seven, and eight years old can learn how to play baseball by joining a Tee Ball team.

You don't have to know how to play Tee Ball already. We have two coaches. They help us learn how to play the game.

The coach shows us how
to hold the bat.

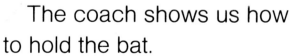

He puts the ball on the hitting tee.

We have to hit the ball as hard as we can. If
we miss or hit the tee, we can try again.

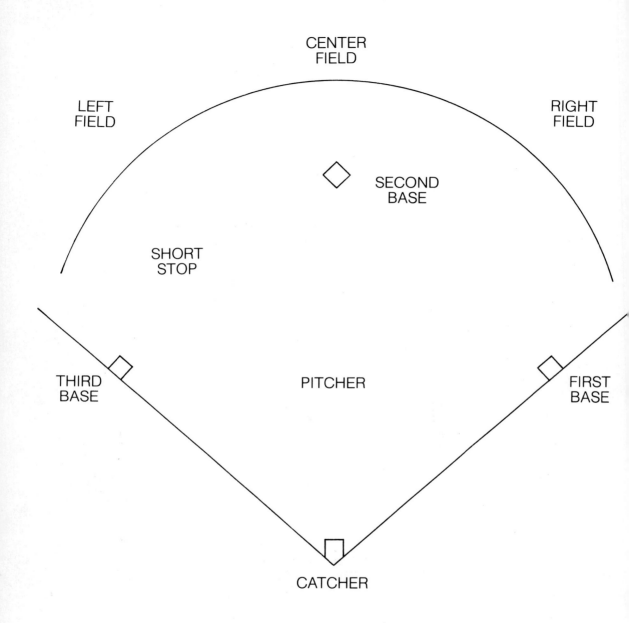

Here is the field we play on. There are nine different positions on our field. That's just like real baseball.

The coach tells us what position we play. We change around during the season, so we learn to play all positions.

The catcher has to wear special equipment, so he or she won't get hurt.

We get team shirts and baseball caps in our team colors.

We play four innings during a game. An inning is when our team bats once and plays the field once.

When it is our turn to bat, the coach tells us who bats first, second, and so on. Each player on our team gets a turn to hit the ball off the tee and out to the field. The other team is on the field.

We wait in the dugout and cheer for our teammate who is up.

It is hard to wait for your turn. But someone always has to bat last.

We cannot go up to bat without a helmet on.

Batter up!

We stand in the batter's box next to the tee and keep our eye on the ball.

Feet apart, elbows up, and then swing!

Oops! Missed it!

Sometimes it is hard to get a hit. We can try again until we hit the ball.

But other times…crack! There it goes! Getting a hit feels great. Everyone cheers!

We have to drop the bat carefully. It is not safe to throw the bat after a hit.

You have to run fast to first base. You have to get there before the ball is caught and thrown to the first baseman.

Safe!

If the first baseman
catches the ball and steps
on the base, you are out.

We can run to the next base when our teammate gets a hit.

Be careful! If the other team catches the ball and tags us, we are out.

The best part is running home. Sometimes we can slide. It is fun!

After our whole team gets a turn at bat, we take our positions on the field.

We learn to catch the ball when it is hit to us. Catching is hard to do. Sometimes we miss.

But we get better and better. When we
catch the ball, we can throw it to a base and
get the other team out.

You have to watch the batter and the ball when it is hit. That ball moves fast!

You have to be quick to stop the ball. It can bounce right through your legs.

In the middle of the season, our coach will pitch to us for an inning or two. That way we learn to hit the ball thrown by a pitcher instead of off the tee. This helps us get ready to play on the bigger teams.

Hitting a pitched ball is very hard. We have to practice. If we miss, we can use the tee.

Smash! That one goes all the way to the fence. A home run! When we hit a home run, we run around and tag all the bases. Coming around all the way to home plate feels great.

By the end of the season, the coach pitches to us every inning. We learn to hit better and better.

In Tee Ball we don't keep score. That way no one has to lose. We can all be winners.

After the game, we line up and shake hands with the other team and say, "Good game! Good game!"

Our coach tells us that we did very well.
We are getting better and better at hitting,
catching, throwing, running, and fielding.

We give our team cheer.

Who are we? "Angels!"
What do we play? "Tee Ball!"
How do we play it? "Gr-r-r-reat!"

Most of all, we have fun!
That's the best thing because
we love Tee Ball.
Everyone wins at Tee Ball!

A NOTE TO PARENTS

Tee Ball is a Little League program designed for youngsters at an early age who want to play baseball or softball. Most youngsters six, seven, and eight years old are not yet able to pitch accurately or to hit a pitched ball. By participating in Tee Ball, they can learn and practice fundamental baseball skills and also receive enjoyment from taking part in a team sport. Using the batting tee, the young player can develop hand-eye coordination and swing techniques without fear of being hit by a pitched ball.

Players are assigned to a team, and play one or two games per week. Games last about an hour and a half and usually are four innings but no more than six. Every inning each player will have the opportunity to hit a fair ball. Protective equipment is required—helmets for all batters and base runners, mask and shin guards and chest protector for the catcher. Uniforms are team shirts and caps.

No score is kept in Tee Ball. Strikes and balls are not called against the batter. A side is retired when all players have had their turn at bat. All games end in a tie.

The purpose of Tee Ball is to learn how to play the game and to have fun. Coaches and managers should be caring and patient in teaching the players about sportsmanship and team play. It can be a rewarding experience. Parents should also have fun watching the games and helping their children succeed at Tee Ball.

NYACK LIBRARY   NYKL

ARY
dway
Nyack, NY 10960

J
796.357 Grosshandler,
GRO   Henry.

         Everyone wins at
         tee ball

$12.95   900014

DATE			

8/90✓ $12.95

NYACK LIBRARY
59 South Broadway
Nyack, NY 10960

© THE BAKER & TAYLOR CO.